DEFINE & DESIGN

STAYING WARM, KEEPING COOL

Linden McNeilly

Rourke
Educational Media

rourkeeducationalmedia.com

Before & After Reading Activities

Before Reading:

Building Academic Vocabulary and Background Knowledge

Before reading a book, it is important to tap into what your child or students already know about the topic. This will help them develop their vocabulary, increase their reading comprehension, and make connections across the curriculum.

1. Look at the cover of the book. What will this book be about?
2. What do you already know about the topic?
3. Let's study the Table of Contents. What will you learn about in the book's chapters?
4. What would you like to learn about this topic? Do you think you might learn about it from this book? Why or why not?
5. Use a reading journal to write about your knowledge of this topic. Record what you already know about the topic and what you hope to learn about the topic.
6. Read the book.
7. In your reading journal, record what you learned about the topic and your response to the book.
8. After reading the book complete the activities below.

Content Area Vocabulary
Read the list. What do these words mean?

breathable
contradictory
efficiency
humidity
inhospitable
membrane
regulating
stroke
textiles
ventilation

After Reading:

Comprehension and Extension Activity

After reading the book, work on the following questions with your child or students in order to check their level of reading comprehension and content mastery.

1. Restate three reasons why engineers design special clothing for harsh weather. (Summarize)
2. Why do you think people feel hotter in humid climates? (Infer)
3. What questions would you ask someone testing a new jacket design? (Asking questions)
4. What things do you do to cool down when you are too warm? (Text to self connection)
5. What questions would you need to answer before you could design a way to keep athletes coo in hot climates? (Asking questions)

Extension Activity

Think of what you like to do when you're outside during the winter. Draw a design of a jacket that would keep you the perfect temperature. Label the features and tell how it's made and what materials you would use to make it.

TABLE OF CONTENTS

Extreme Weather Demands
Extreme Clothing.. 4
Working in Winter Conditions 6
How Smart is Your Clothing?................... 12
Clothing That Can Breathe 14
Beat the Heat 18
Plastic Wrap? No Sweat! 21
Firefighters Keep Their Cool................... 24
Glossary.. 30
Index 31
Show What You Know 31
Websites to Visit..................................... 31
About the Author 32

EXTREME WEATHER

People in harsh conditions need special clothing. Firefighters require protection from heat. Oil industry workers in the Arctic must stay warm. Active people in extreme climates want clothing that helps protect them.

People need the right temperature—not too hot and not too cold—for a high level of comfort. Engineers are working in different parts of the world to design **textiles** to make into clothing that meets these needs.

DEMANDS EXTREME CLOTHING

Bears That Don't Go *Brrrrr!*
Polar bears living in sub-zero temperatures have oily hairs that keep water out and hollow hairs that trap air. Their fat acts as another layer to keep cold away.

WORKING IN WINTER CONDITIONS

Designing work clothing for Arctic conditions is tough. Workers in the oil and gas industry do many things in this **inhospitable** climate. They spend much of their time outside enduring wind, rain, and snow. They climb and hang from harnesses.

Sometimes they wear hearing protection and facemasks, and need quick access to communication devices. They go from being very physical to staying still, which makes **regulating** body temperatures very tricky.

Feel the Breeze—Not the Cold

Heated vests can plug into a motorcycle's electrical system to give riders just the right amount of warmth without being too constricting. The lightweight, tightly woven fabric keeps out the wind, too.

This driller needs clothing that protects him while also allowing easy movement.

An international clothing designer, Wenaas, partnered with SINTEF, a research firm, to find Arctic clothing solutions. They interviewed workers to find out what they needed on the job and used the data they collected to aid their design.

Arctic winters can be as cold as -30 degrees Fahrenheit (-34 degrees Celsius). The short summers only warm to a high of 54 degrees Fahrenheit (12 degrees Celsius).

SINTEF researcher Ole Petter Naesgaard says that designing appropriate clothing for these workers calls for **contradictory** requirements. It has to be light enough to move freely, yet provide a barrier to fierce wind, moisture, and below freezing temperatures. Since workers move a lot, their suits must stay cool despite sweating.

Warm Legs Make a Warm Body

Since legs aren't very sensitive to cold, you may not realize that losing heat from your legs is common. Keeping your legs warm is as important as wearing a hat.

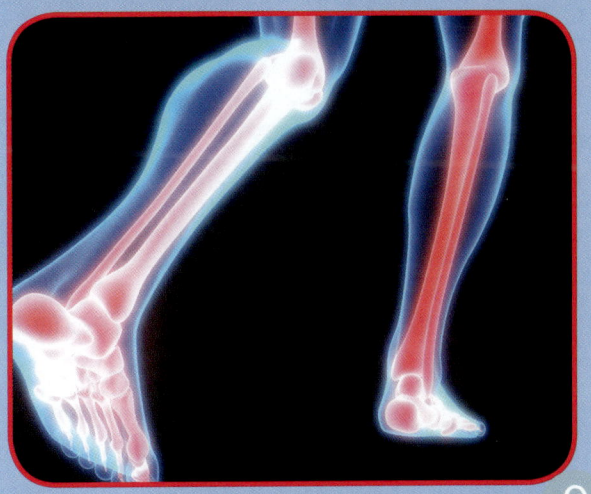

Their solution is several specialized layers. The first is woolen underwear, which has fireproof qualities and keeps in warmth. The next layer is like fleece, with soft, puffy fibers specially designed to hold a lot of air for both warmth and **ventilation**. The outer layer is waterproof and **breathable**, with proper coverage of the legs.

Natural and synthetic fleece trap air between the material's fibers, which is what makes it so warm.

Special gloves have extra padding around the knuckles and a curve that helps grip in cold conditions. Laboratories using both dummies and humans test the designs.

Test Labs Put People Through the Paces
Occupational physiology labs test new products thoroughly. This lab's equipment tests how a person's lungs and heart function while using the product. It also measures the effect on body temperature.

HOW SMART IS YOUR CLOTHING?

Dressing smart is one thing, but what if the clothing itself had brains? Norwegian laboratories are testing the concept of intelligent clothing. The jackets incorporate sensors that check and report on the physical state of the wearer as well as the weather outside.

The sensors measure how the body responds during activity and rest during extreme weather conditions. If the body is too stressed, warnings are relayed to a monitor.

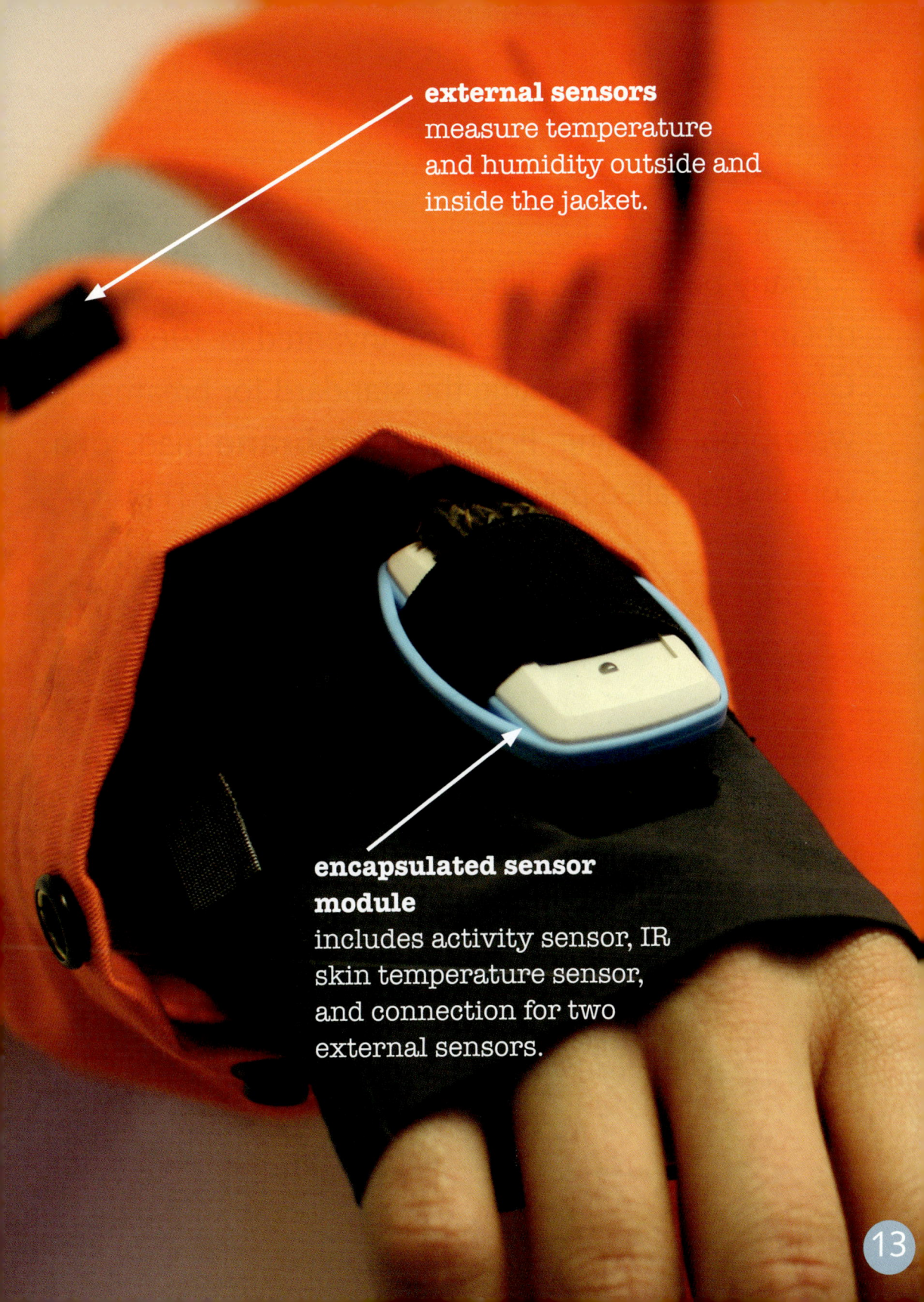

external sensors
measure temperature and humidity outside and inside the jacket.

encapsulated sensor module
includes activity sensor, IR skin temperature sensor, and connection for two external sensors.

CLOTHING THAT CAN BREATHE

Many outdoor clothing companies use some form of Gore-Tex™ in their textiles. Invented in 1969, Gore-Tex quickly became the standard for breathable, waterproof clothing. It uses a **membrane** made of a compound called polytetrafluoroethylene (PTFE).

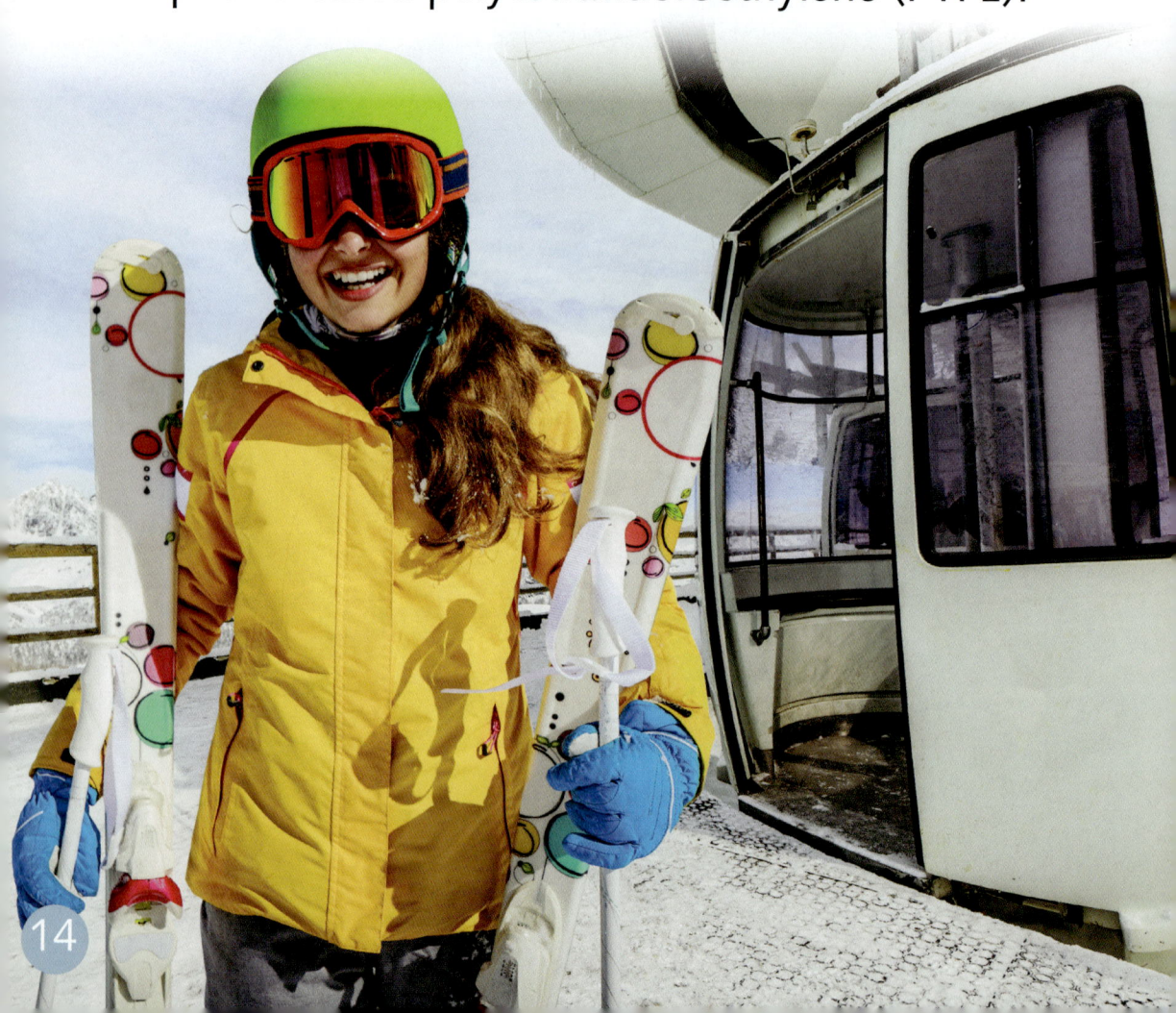

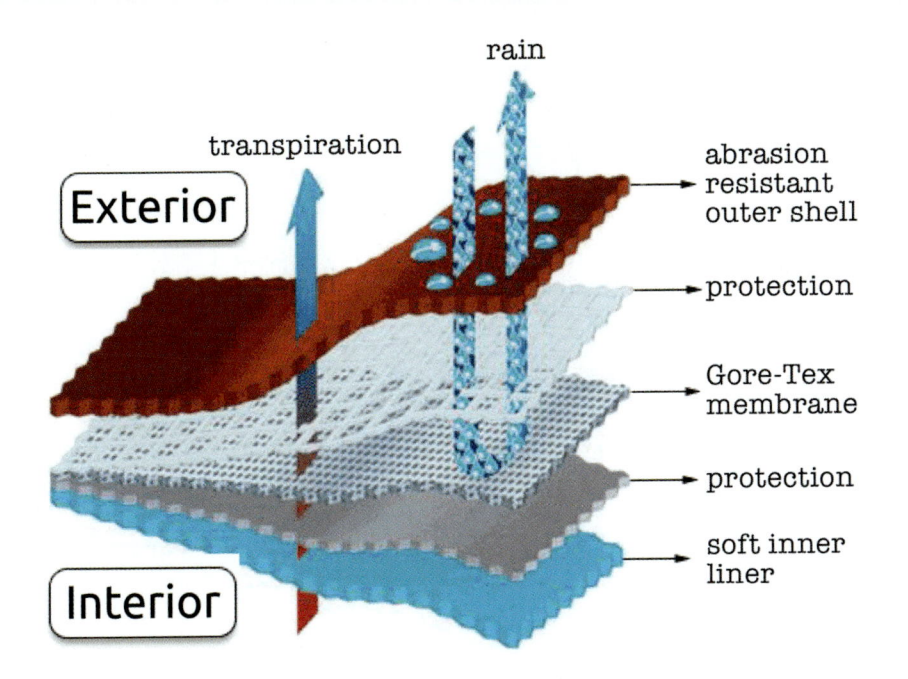

Diagram labels:
- rain
- transpiration
- Exterior
- Interior
- abrasion resistant outer shell
- protection
- Gore-Tex membrane
- protection
- soft inner liner

Most companies laminate the membrane to an outer shell, sometimes stitch over the seams and add another layer underneath for comfort. All this layering adds bulk and makes the garment hard to use in highly physical situations.

Fabric That Breathes
When PTFE is stretched into a thin membrane, its pores are too small for water drops to enter but large enough for sweat vapor to pass through, making it waterproof and breathable.

15

Maker Project

Cup Cozy

Winter means a cup of something warm—but not if it goes cold quickly! This cozy uses thermal insulation to keep your drink warm.

Tools and Parts:

- Paper
- Glue gun
- Scissors

- Self-adhesive Velcro, 2 inches by 1 inch (5.08 cm by 2.54 cm)
- 2 pieces cotton fabric, 4.5 inches by 12 inches (11 cm by 30 cm)
- 1 piece of packing foam sheet, 1/8 inch (.32 cm) thick, 4.5 inches by 12 inches (11 cm by 30 cm) long
- Reusable cup for hot liquids

Steps:

1. Design your cup cozy shape. Use either an arc to fit snuggly against the cup or a rectangle if your cup does not taper at the bottom. Test your shape on your cup. It needs to wrap around your cup with the ends overlapping at least 1.5 inches (3.81 cm).

2. Make a paper pattern of your cozy, adding 1/4 inch (.635 cm) on all sides. Cut it out.

3. Use the pattern to cut out the two pieces of cotton and the foam.

4. Trim the foam so that it's about 1/4 inch (.635 cm) smaller than the cotton fabric on all sides.

5. Place one piece of cotton with printed side down. Position the air foam on top, leaving equal space around all sides.

6. Carefully put a line of hot glue at the very edge of the fabric on all sides.

7. Lay the second piece of fabric print side up, matching the edges and smoothing out the glue underneath so it closes in the air foam. Let cool.

8. Separate the two Velcro parts. Stick one part vertically along the end. Do the same to the matching Velcro on the other end, but on the underside of the fabric.

9. Wrap your hot cup and stay cozy!

Why Wool Works When It's Wet

Fine wool fibers trap air. When they absorb sweat, the chemical bonds between the wool and water release energy that gives off heat. You stay warm, even when you're wet.

BEAT THE HEAT

What if the environment is hot rather than cold? Hot climates are trickier, because heat is harder to avoid than cold. In hot climates, body temperatures can quickly soar, leading to heat stroke and collapse.

Fabric that opens and closes like pinecones
Researchers at the London College of Fashion and Bath University want to design fabric with tiny spikes that open when it's hot and close down to trap air when it's cold.

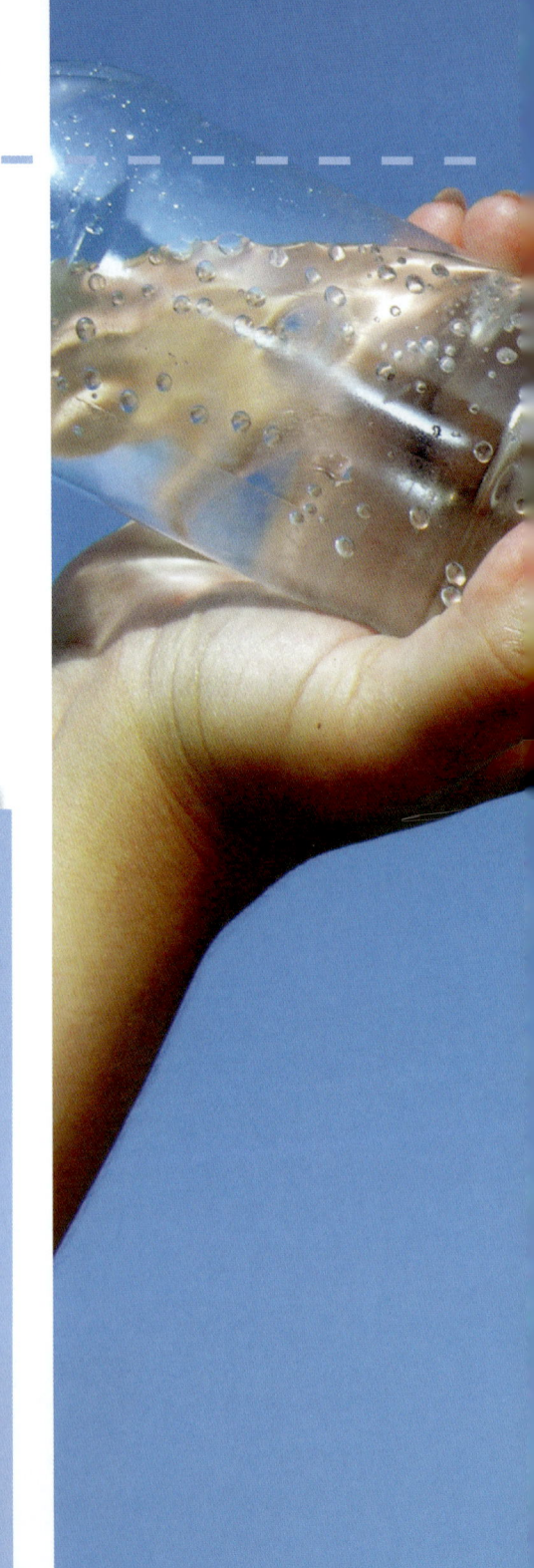

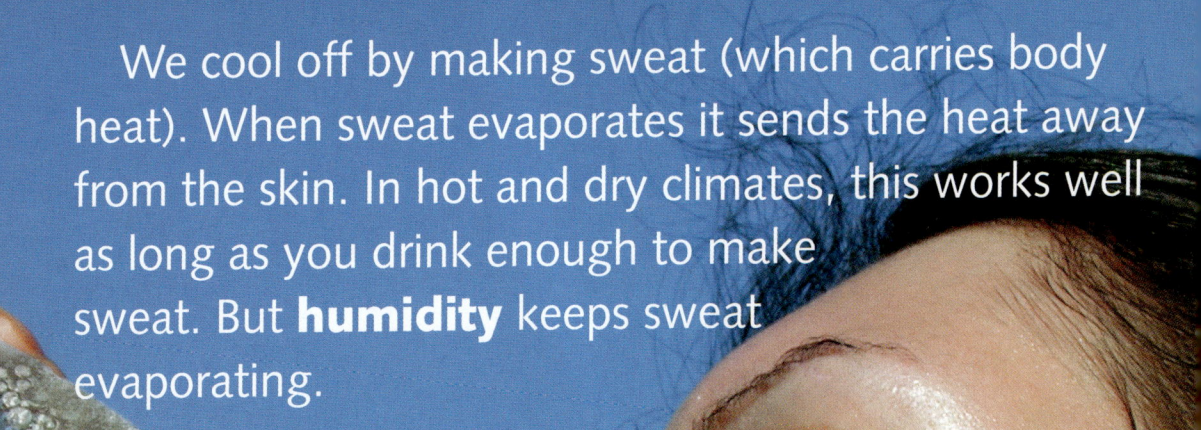

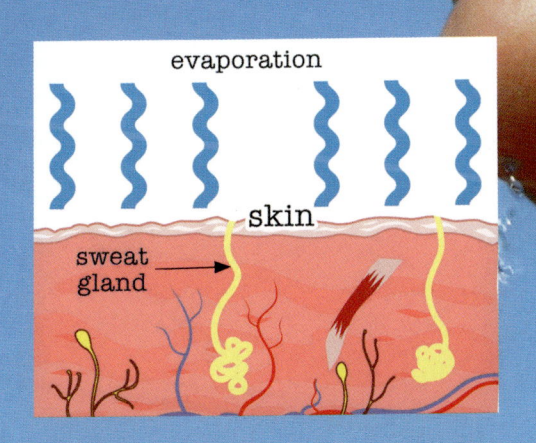

We cool off by making sweat (which carries body heat). When sweat evaporates it sends the heat away from the skin. In hot and dry climates, this works well as long as you drink enough to make sweat. But **humidity** keeps sweat evaporating.

Sweat glands release moisture that's evaporated, taking the heat with it.

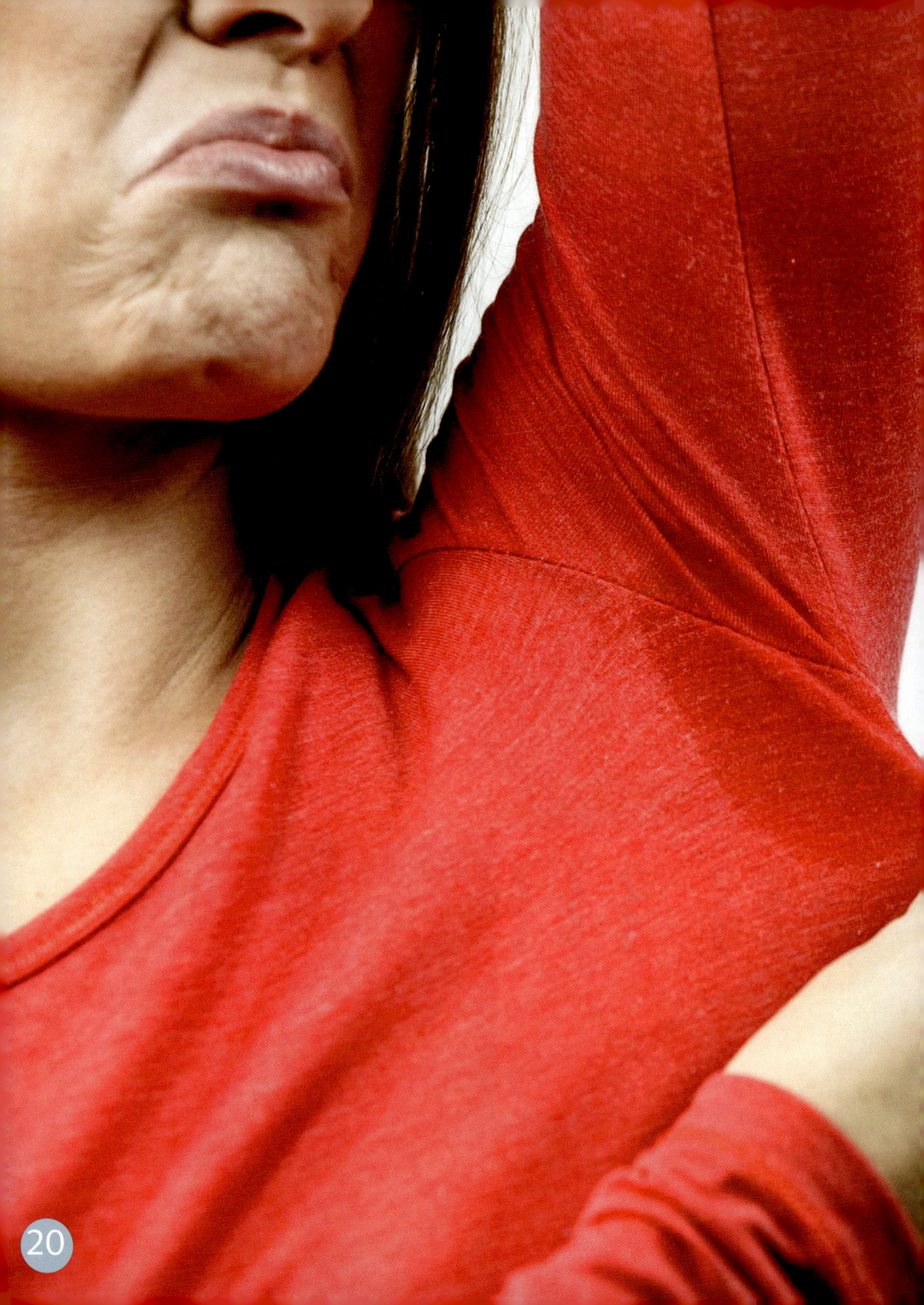

PLASTIC WRAP? NO SWEAT!

Some fabrics make you feel even hotter by trapping sweat close to the skin. But what if we could wear clothing that lets both sweat and heat escape? Cooler skin could mean less need for air-conditioning, lowering energy costs.

Stanford engineers think they have a solution: a plastic-based textile with properties that cool down the skin. They used polyethylene, otherwise known as kitchen plastic wrap, and engineered features to make it suitable to clothing.

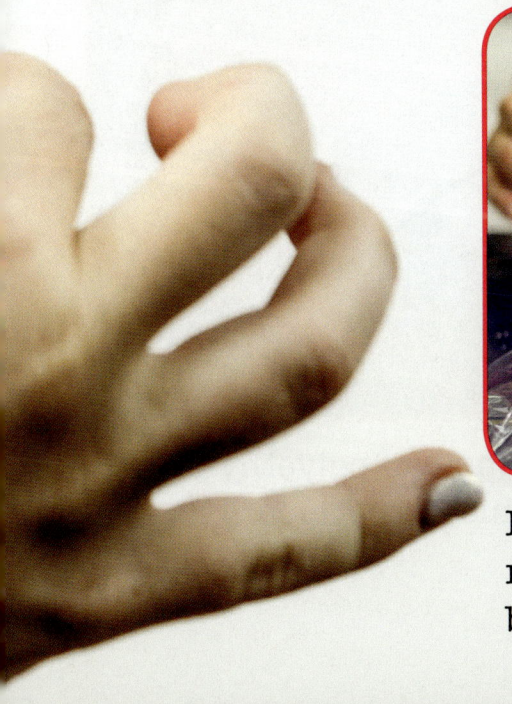

Plastic wrap usually keeps moisture and heat in, so it must be changed to let them escape.

First, they found a kind of polyethylene used in battery-making that lets heat out but isn't see-through. Then, they changed it chemically so that water vapor molecules—like sweat—could escape. The result was a paper-thin, plastic fabric that could breathe.

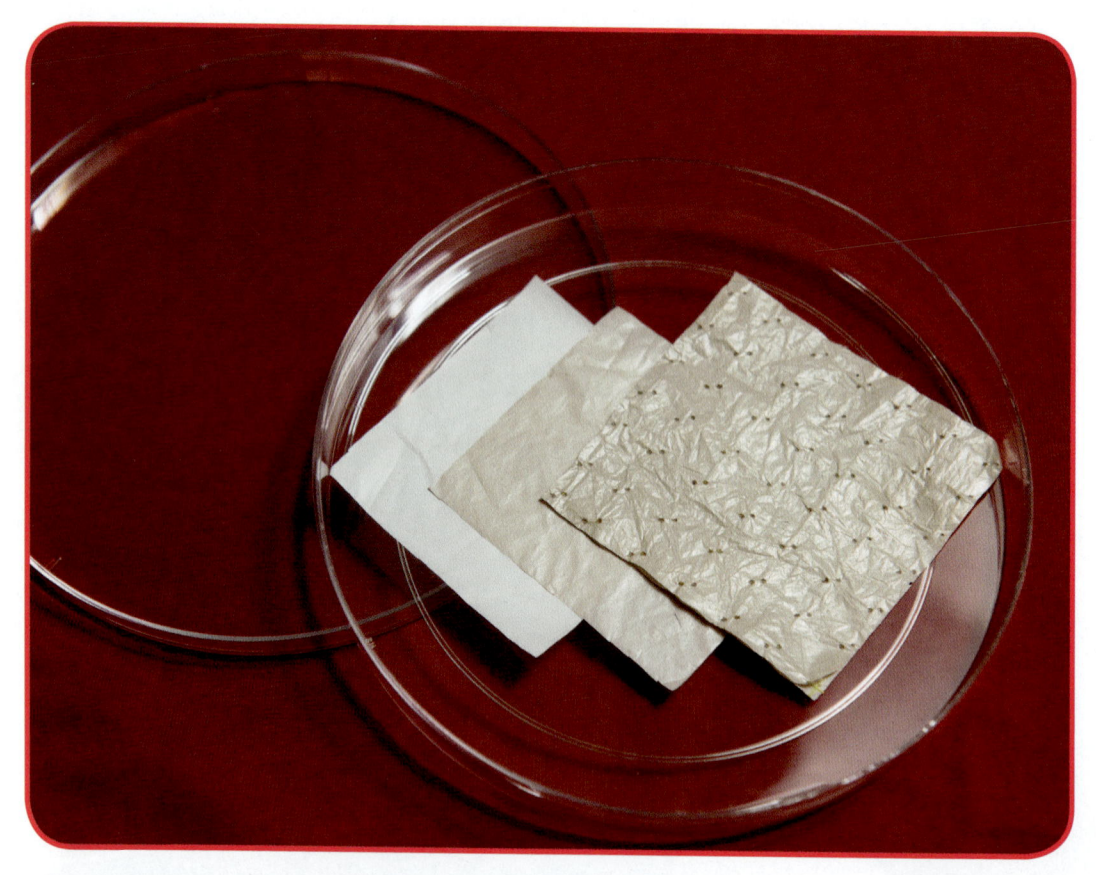

Stanford researchers began with a sheet of polyethylene and modified it with a series of chemical treatments, resulting in a cooling fabric.

Engineers sandwiched cotton mesh between two sheets of this specialized fabric to make a stronger, thicker fabric. In tests against plain cotton fabric the newly designed fabric left surface skin temperatures 3.6 degrees Fahrenheit (-15.8 degrees Celsius) lower.

Heat That's Really Light

Our bodies throw off heat in a form of light called infrared radiation, which humans can see only with night-vision goggles. Controlling how textiles allow heat to escape is the key to cooling fabrics.

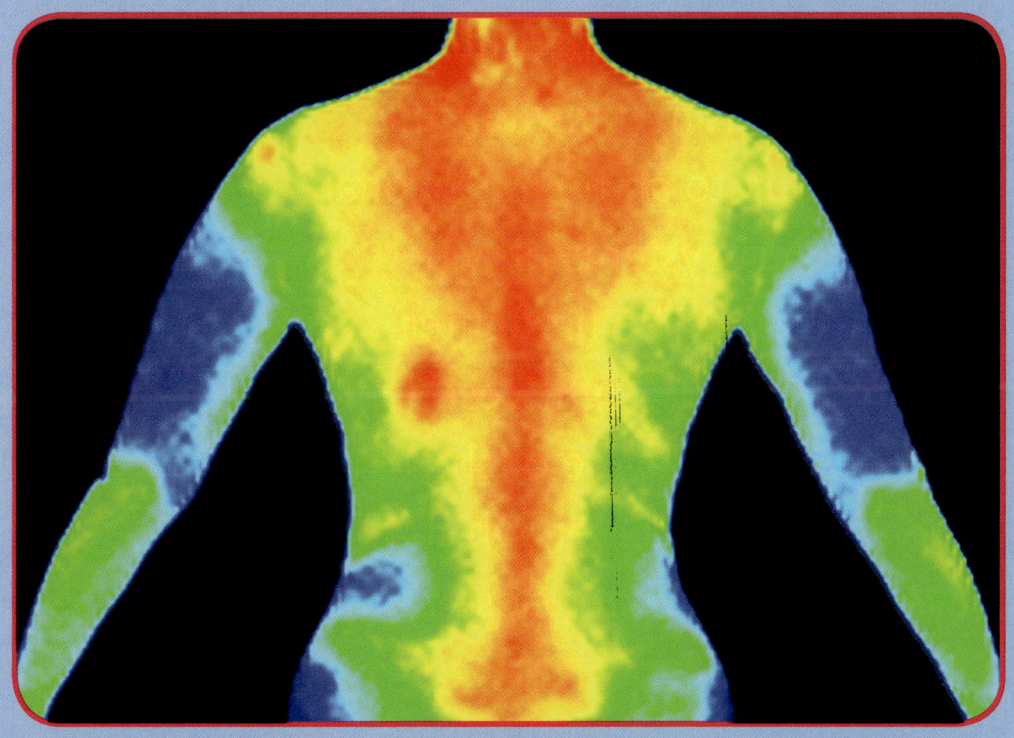

FIREFIGHTERS KEEP THEIR COOL

When leaving a burning building, firefighters' core temperatures can range from 122 to 125 degrees Fahrenheit (50 to 51.6 degrees Celsius). Those temperatures must come down as quickly to prevent a **stroke** or a heart attack.

During breaks, firefighters can cool down using fans. But this can take up to an hour. Personal cooling vest systems provide quicker relief. The firefighter wears the lightweight vest during work. On breaks, he or she plugs the vest into a cooler, which circulates cold water close to the body's core.

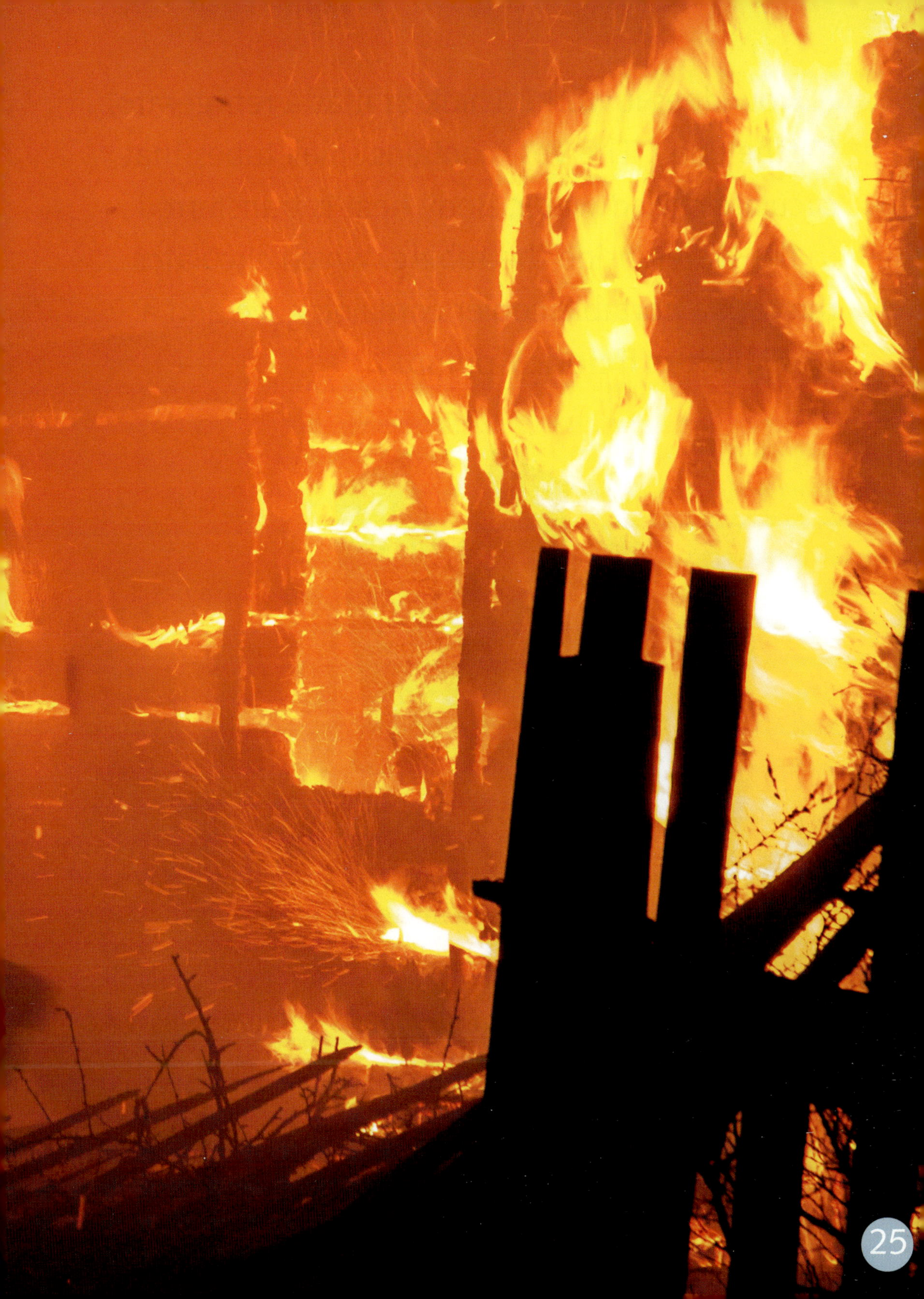

How does it work? Think of it as a refrigerator for the body. The vest contains small tubes that circulate chilled water. Body heat is transferred to the water inside the tubing, which circulates through a portable cooler containing ice and a small high-**efficiency** pump.

Cooling vests are an important part of a firefighter's gear. In some instances, they could make the difference between life and death.

The absorbed heat slowly melts the ice, keeping the temperature of the water constant until all of the ice has melted. For more cooling, you can add ice.

This cooler has a water port panel that can connect to several cooling vests at once.

Sweaty Hunters Bag the Game

Historically, our ability to sweat kept us cooler than other animals. Early humans could hunt game during the hottest parts of the day, when other predators were forced to rest.

Athletes use similar methods to maintain healthy body temperature with cooling wrist bands. When you put the Aqua Coolkeeper™ in water, the specially developed HydroQuartz™ inside forms a cooling gel. The gel absorbs body heat and releases this heat through evaporation.

Engineers Find Solutions

No matter the weather, engineers are looking for ways to make the right clothing for the activities we do. Whether it's hot or cold, windy or wet, a designer somewhere is thinking of solutions to cover, cool, and keep us comfortable.

Those Who Can't Sweat, Poop! Some storks and vultures use liquid to cool off, but it isn't sweat. They let very wet poop fall on their legs, and when it dries off, heat is carried away.

Maker Project

Cooling Neck Scarf

Cooling your neck helps you stay comfortable on hot days. This scarf uses evaporation to cool where your blood is close to the surface.

Tools and Parts:

- Cotton fabric, 4 inches by 32 inches (10 by 81 centimeters)
- Sewing machine
- Iron
- Pencil
- Water absorbing polymer crystals

Steps:

1. Fold fabric in half lengthwise, right sides together. Using a 1/4 inch (.635 centimeter) seam, stitch down each end, turning at corner and stitching for 10 inches (25.4 centimeters) on long edge. Do the same thing on the other end, stitching down from fold, turning corner until seam is 10 inches (25.4 centimeters) long. There should be a 12-inch (30.48-centimeter) gap along middle of cut edge left.

2. Turn tube right side out. Fold under 1/4 inch (.635 centimeter) unsewn edge. Press. Lay out horizontally.

3. Make vertical seams from open edge to fold, measuring from the left end at the following points: 10, 14, 18, and 22 inches (25, 35, 45, and 60 centimeters).

4. Put a teaspoon of crystals in three open sections. Stitch across the open edge.

5. To use: soak in water until crystals swell. Wear tied around neck.

6. When crystals dry up, they can be soaked and used again and again.

GLOSSARY

breathable (BREETH-ay-buhl): having the quality of allowing air through

contradictory (kahn-truh-DIK-tur-ee): opposite, contrary or not consistent

efficiency (i-FISH-uhn-see): the quality of working or operating well, quickly and without waste

humidity (hyoo-MID-i-tee): the amount of moisture in the air

inhospitable (in-HAH-spi-tuh-buhl): not friendly, welcoming or generous

membrane (MEM-brane): a very thin layer of plastic or other material that protects something

regulating (REG-yuh-late-ing): keeping something at some standard

stroke (strohk): a sudden lack of oxygen in part of the brain

textiles (TEK-stilez): woven or knitted fabrics or cloth

ventilation (ven-tuh-LAY-shuhn): system for fresh air coming in and stale air going out

INDEX

breathable   10
efficiency   26
fleece   10
humidity   13, 19
infrared radiation   23
inhospitable   6
membrane   14

occupational physiology   11
polyethylene   21, 22
regulating   6
textiles   4
vapor   15, 22
ventilation   10

SHOW WHAT YOU KNOW

1. Why is it difficult to find the right clothing for those who work outdoors in the Arctic?
2. Why is it important to test new clothing designs in labs?
3. Why should active clothing be able to breathe?
4. How does sweat cool you down?
5. Why do firefighters need breaks?

WEBSITES TO VISIT

www.sciencekids.co.nz/
http://www.explainthatstuff.com/
http://www.sciencebuddies.org/

ABOUT THE AUTHOR

Linden McNeilly is a writer who taught public school for many years. She writes books about science, history and art, including books on bugs you can eat, art you can make with maps, and twelve different views on the Great Depression. She lives with her family and a bunch of pets in the redwoods in the Central Coast of California. Visit her at www.lindenmcneilly.com

Meet The Author!
www.meetREMauthors.com

© 2018 Rourke Educational Media

All rights reserved. No part of this book may be reproduced or utilized in any form or by any means, electronic or mechanical including photocopying, recording, or by any information storage and retrieval system without permission in writing from the publisher.

www.rourkeeducationalmedia.com

PHOTO CREDITS: Cover: hikers © Zhuk Roman, firefighters © Blue Sky Studio, logo elements: lightbulb © Alfazet Chronicles, circuit board © Vector.design; gears © RedlineVector; pages 4-5 © firefighters VAKSMAN VOLODYMYR, snow hikers © yurii.repalo, polar bear © Alexey Seafarer; page 6 vests © Aerostitch; page 7 © NOAA Climate Program Office, NABOS 2006 Expedition., page 8-9 © Nordroden, page 9 © Magic mine; page 11 treadmill © Photographee.eu; fleece © Cgoodwin https://creativecommons.org/licenses/by/3.0/deed.en; page 12-13 © SINTEF; page 14-15 GoreTex logo on fabric © GROGL, illustration © Solipsist https://creativecommons.org/licenses/by-sa/3.0/deed.en , 14-15 skier © gorillaimages; page 17 wool © Stacey Newman; page 18-19 girl © yuris, open pine cone © Chromakey, closed pine cone © Protasov AN, skin diagram © Refluo; page 20 plastic wrap © Jarib, woman in red shirt © Voyagerix; page 22 © Linda A. Cicero / Stanford News Service, page 23 infrared radiation © Anita van den Broek; page 24-25 © Jackan, page 26 and 27 © COOLSHIRT SYSTEMS, page 27 cavemen © By Nicolas Primola; page 28 stork © putneymark   https://creativecommons.org/licenses/by-sa/2.0/deed.en

Edited by: Keli Sipperley

Cover and Interior design by: Nicola Stratford   www.nicolastratford.com

Library of Congress PCN Data

Staying Warm, Keeping Cool / Linden McNeilly
 (Define and Design)
  ISBN 978-1-68342-355-3 (hard cover)
  ISBN 978-1-68342-451-2 (soft cover)
  ISBN 978-1-68342-521-2 (e-Book)
Library of Congress Control Number: 2017931198

Rourke Educational Media
Printed in the United States of America, North Mankato, Minnesota